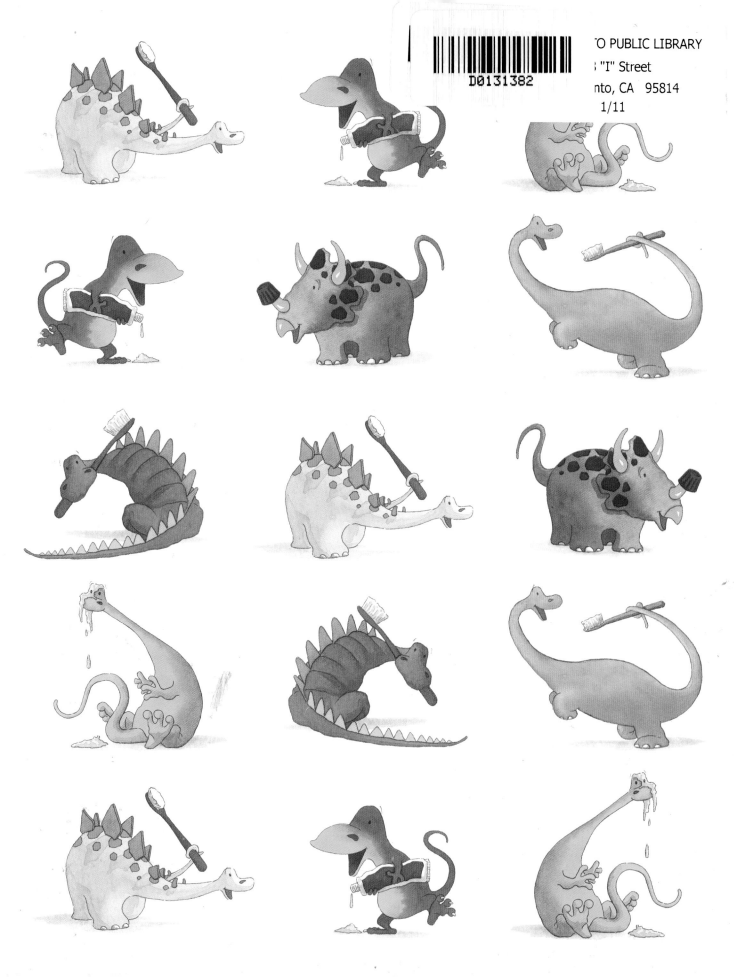

For Jack Drake,
my favorite dentist
—I.W.

For Mr. Jon Harris,
who is a good brusher
—A.R.

Text copyright © 2001 by Ian Whybrow
Illustrations copyright © 2001 by Adrian Reynolds
All rights reserved under International and Pan-American Copyright Conventions.
First published in the United States by Random House Children's Books,
a division of Random House, Inc., New York, in 2004.
First published in Great Britain by Gullane Children's Books in 2001
and subsequently by Puffin Books in 2003.
www.randomhouse.com/kids
Library of Congress Cataloging-in-Publication Data
Whybrow, Ian. Harry and the dinosaurs say "Raahh!" /
by Ian Whybrow ; illustrated by Adrian Reynolds. — 1st Random House ed.
p. cm.
SUMMARY: A young boy takes his toy dinosaurs with him to help calm his
fears on his first visit to the dentist.
ISBN 0-375-82542-8
[1. Dentists—Fiction. 2. Dinosaurs—Fiction. 3. Toys—Fiction.]
I. Reynolds, Adrian, ill. II. Title.
PZ7.W6225 Hap 2004 [E]—dc21
2003001480
PRINTED IN CHINA First American Edition 10 9 8 7 6 5 4 3 2 1
RANDOM HOUSE and colophon are registered trademarks of Random House, Inc.

Harry *and the* Dinosaurs *say* "Raahh!"

Written by **Ian Whybrow**
Illustrated by **Adrian Reynolds**

Random House ⌂ New York

Mom had her coat on,
but Harry was being slow.
They were going to see
Dr. Drake, the dentist.

Harry was only a bit scared.
That was because of Sam showing
him her filling.

Harry wanted to take his dinosaurs,
but they were hiding all over the place.
He called all their names.

He said, "Get in the bucket, my Stegosaurus."
And out came Stegosaurus from under the pillow.

He said, "Get in the bucket, my Triceratops."
And out came Triceratops from inside the drawer.

And one by one, Apatosaurus and Scelidosaurus
and Anchisaurus all came out of their hiding
places and they jumped into the bucket.

All except for Tyrannosaurus. He didn't want
to go because he had a lot of teeth. He thought
Dr. Drake might do drilling on them.

Harry said, "Don't worry, because when we get there, I shall press a magic button on my bucket, and that will make you grow big."

In the waiting room, the nurse said,
"Hello, Harry. Are you a good boy?"
Harry said, "I am, but my dinosaurs bite."

Then Dr. Drake called,
"Next, please!"

The nurse took Harry into Dr. Drake's room.
Harry wasn't sure about the big chair. He thought
maybe that was where Dr. Drake did the drilling.
    "Come and have a ride in my chair," said Dr. Drake.
"It goes up and down."
    Harry didn't want to ride.
    "Would one of your dinosaurs like a turn?"
asked Dr. Drake.

Harry put Tyrannosaurus on the chair.
He whispered to him not to worry.
Then he pressed the magic button. . . .
Tyrannosaurus grew VERY BIG!

"Open wide," said Dr. Drake,
and then he turned around. . . .

"RAAAAHH!" said Tyrannosaurus.
"Help!" cried Dr. Drake, hiding behind
the door. "Harry, what shall I do?"

Harry pressed the magic button.
Tyrannosaurus went right back
to being bucket-sized.

Harry felt safer now about getting
into the chair, so he climbed in with
his bucket. Then Harry and his dinosaurs
all had a ride together.

They opened their mouths wide for
Dr. Drake, and all went, "RAAAAHH!"

Dr. Drake said, "What a lot of teeth!
Will they bite me?"

Harry said, "They only bite drills."

"You are all good brushers," said Dr. Drake,
"so no drills today, only a look and a rinse."

All the dinosaurs liked riding and they liked rinsing.
"Another bucket of mouthwash, Joan!" called
Dr. Drake.

Going home, Mom let Harry choose a book
from the library for being so good.
   "Let's have a shark book!" said Harry.
   "RAAAAHH!" said the dinosaurs.
   "Sharp teeth! We like sharks!"

ENDOSAURUS